Awakened
by Surprise

For Russell and his fictional surprises in WWGB,

Pax,

Awakened by Surprise

Roberto Bonazzi
Robert Bonazzi
2016

Literary Press
LAMAR UNIVERSITY

Copyright © 2016 Robert Bonazzi
All rights reserved.

ISBN: 978-1-942956-17-4
Library of Congress Control Number: 2016933542

Collages by Maggi Miller
Manufactured in the United States of America

Lamar University Literary Press
Beaumont, Texas

For Russell Hardin
and to the memory of
Daniel L. Robertson

Books by Robert Bonazzi

Outside the Margins: Literary Commentaries
Man in the Mirror: The Story of Black Like Me
The Scribbling Cure: Poems & Prose Poems
Maestro of Solitude: Poems & Poetics
Perpetual Texts: Poetic Sequences
Fictive Music: Prose Poems
Living the Borrowed Life: Poems
Domingo, Poems with Carlos Isla &
C.W. Truesdale, (Spanish/English)

Acknowledgments

Earlier versions appeared in *Transatlantic Review* (London), *TriQuarterly, Granite, The Village Voice, New Letters, Minnesota Review, Lillabulero, Duende, New Orleans Review, Gallimaufry, Mississippi Review, Center, Excelsior* (Mexico City), and in these anthologies: *Tales of Austin, Plaza of Encounters*, and *Extreme Unctions and Other Last Rites*.

Other Fiction from Lamar University Literary Press

David Bowles, *Border Lore*
Kevin K. Casey, *Four-Peace*
Gerald Duff, *Memphis Mojo*
Gretchen Johnson, *The Joy of Deception*
Christopher Linforth, *When You Find Us We Will Be Gone*
Tom Mack and Andrew Geyer, editors, *A Shared Voice*
Harold Raley, *Louisiana Rogue*
Jim Sanderson, *Trashy Behavior*
Jan Seale, *Appearances*
Melvin Sterne, *The Number You Have Reached*
John Wegner, *Love Is not a Dirty Word*
Robert Wexelblatt, *The Artist Wears Rough Clothing*

For more information about these and other books, go to
www.lamar.edu/literarypress

CONTENTS

11   Creative Agitation

Awakened by Surprise

15   Caretaker of the Estate
21   A Faded Mosaic
27   Maximinutiae
31   Aesthetics of Waste
37   Window Panes
41   Guards
45   Novel Bridge
49   A Dream of Footsteps
53   Bagatelles
55   Twilight Texts

Howling at the Moon

65   The Idea of Coffee
69   Philosophical Reflections
77   The Musical Erotic

Creative Agitation

Success is the beginning of failure.
Fame is the beginning of disgrace.
   —Chuang Tzu
    Translated by Thomas Merton

  Immersed in speculation, this collection believes in two ideas—that the serious *and* the comic carry equal weight and that fragmentary illuminations can reveal the creative agitation of an inner life. Writing since the early 1960s, when I first believed in becoming an author, these earliest works were efforts to tell a story, although I possessed no gift for storytelling. The most "successful" was an imagined account of my late twin brother's time as a medic in Vietnam. "Light Casualties" was published in *Transatlantic Review*, a London literary magazine in 1968, and cited by *Best American Short Stories* and *Vietnam War Literature*. That story turned out to be my last attempt at reading the world in a conventional way. Soon after, I abandoned realism for comic absurdity, which seems closer to reality.

  Portions of the first "experimental" novella—*Howling at the Moon* (a take-off on Kierkegaard's *Either/Or*)—were published in anthologies and magazines, including a translation into Spanish by Linda Scheer that was in Mexico City's *Excelsior*, but these "tall tales" appear here for the first time under one roof.

  Later fictions ("A Faded Mosaic," "Maximinutiae" and "Twilight Texts") were assembled from fragments during the past few years for personal amusement, but were never submitted to periodicals. Since my fifties, I have sent work out *only* when it was requested. I never entered a "creative writing" mill, but as an English major completed the course work for a master's degree (never writing a thesis). I taught freshman English classes at the University of Houston on a meager graduate fellowship, but chose not to pursue an academic career. Yet in order to survive, I have taught at universities, community colleges, and in public schools, written and lectured on the life and work of John Howard Griffin, and read poetry in the lively, marginal spaces that still exist within our withering culture.

Fame is elsewhere, usually in a glossy format, but where does wisdom reside? I have *not* learned wisdom from successes, except to know that they were accidents—not that the failures were committed on purpose. I have *not* won any literary prizes or grants (except as the editor/publisher of Latitudes Press, 1966-2000), coming close only once, when *Maestro of Solitude*, a book of poems and poetics (Wings Press, 2005) was among three nominees for the Texas Institute of Letters poetry award. It did not win. I have experienced no success in any conventional sense. Every business or project I began failed, including an after hours club, a print shop, a typesetting service, three literary magazines, and an independent literary imprint.

Part of experience becomes grounded in where and with whom one lives—wives or lady friends, or alone with cats. While I adhere truthfully to what I remember in personal essays, other experiences (often about unnamed women) have evolved into some of these fictions.

Awakened by Surprise

Language is like a cracked kettle on which we beat out tunes for bears to dance to, while all the time we long to move the stars to pity.   —Gustav Flaubert

What is new exists without being progress. Everything is in the effect of surprise. Surprise is the greatest source of what is new.   —Guillaume Apollinaire

Caretaker of the Estate

I

I'm not a violent man yet I have this pistol. They've issued this pistol to me, or left it in my care. It's supposed to be in my possession at all times. I'm the caretaker of the estate, or the pistol is the caretaker of the estate and I'm the caretaker of it. But I take no care of the pistol—never clean or oil it. It's not loaded, never keep it loaded. When it was issued years ago, I went directly to the cottage, unloaded six chambers, counted six cartridges, and rechecked the chambers—all empty. I swore I'd never reload it. Who knows if I might have a mad impulse to fire it?

I keep the pistol hidden in a large pocket of my jacket. The pistol bulges no more than my field glasses in the other pocket. I switch them from pocket to pocket at random, sometimes forgetting which holds the pistol. Reaching for the field glasses to watch a wild rabbit or birds migrating toward the ocean, I sometimes draw out the pistol by mistake. It used to startle me, but now I calmly slide it into the empty pocket.

Back in the cottage at night, I caress my notebook as if it were a woman. I write so hard that when a page is turned I can see deep impressions from the other side. That is, writing on the front of the page gives the back of each page memory. I can't even turn a page on myself. I pursue myself—relentlessly.

I'm a passionate man, although it's not as evident as it once was. The gardener is passionate about his garden, the housekeeper seems to be passionate about beating the rugs from the mansion, and they have been passionate together. During the day they ignore each other, giving no hint about their passion. But it's my duty to know what goes on day and night. I tour the grounds at odd hours. I've seen them by lamplight, heard them through the thin walls, but they don't know I've heard their lovemaking. Not that I go out of my way to hear it. It's not what I would call melodic— his grunting and spitting in alternation with her choking and sighing. I've listened only when some unusual sound had drawn me toward their quarters. Sounds travel great distances here on cold clear nights.

II

It takes years to recognize all the faces in a beautiful face. We notice the pretty faces immediately and forget them. Then interesting faces, which strike strangely at odd angles and surprise at unexpected distances. Many tawdry faces that seem corrupt. Then the ugly ones that can be such sad faces—beautiful for a moment.

I have to go now.
Don't go.
This could go on forever, but it must end.
Why?
I don't want to get into it more deeply.
What is it you fear?
I'm not afraid of it, but of the deprivation once I let go.

Remembered glimpses of faces once memorized. Bodies known intimately. I've lost my touch, imagining a voice I can't hear. Her scent gone from under fingernails.

I've felt possessed for years, but now I know who you are.

No, but you come close to knowing.

If I don't know, I don't want to know. It's just too sad.

But what if the unknown is the happier part?

I can't know that for sure.

And if you could?

How is that we are absolutely alone? Do our skins hold us in? No matter what we do or how close we come, no matter how I push this piece of matter inside that piece of matter—we remain absolutely alone.

You came at the right time, for I may have ignored you earlier.

I knew that. That's why I stayed away.

Good instincts.

As you've always said.

But I haven't forgotten that you've left many times.

And I've come back one more time than I left.

III

Then one morning she left while I slept. I awakened to her scribbled note, complaining about what she perceived as my fear of intimacy. I do not fear intimacy itself, but only what happens when one talks about it. And the words spoken after it's over. Such bathetic blather demeans all that was exquisitely pleasurable. What will finally destroy the desire for too much will be the chattering on about it. This intense need to relive one's intimacy in words always self-destructs. Those lovely moments of experience should consume themselves without one word.

In truth, I'm not the caretaker of the estate, nor do I possess a pistol. Yes, I've been assigned to this cottage, just as others were assigned. The gardener and housekeeper exist with real names, but I've only imagined their lovemaking.

I live under a ceiling of tightly woven palm leaves—an intricate underside that's still pale green, but outside the roof looks like straw. The estate mansion has a slate roof, marble walls, and tile floors; its windows are tall and glistening. My walls are adobe, with a floor of dirt and straw, and windows with wooden shutters but no screens. I've learned to check my clothes and shoes for scorpions.

On my roof lives a reptile called the *besucon*—similar to an iguana but much smaller. It has a peculiar call, a guttural chirping sound. I thought it was a bird when I first heard it. It calls about every ten minutes in a consistent rhythm. I don't time it. I don't know if it's male or female or if there's a pair or many, but the calls seems always the same. If there's only one it never sleeps, or sleeps only when I do. If there are many, they never call out at the same time or closer than ten minutes apart.

I assume their calls are only for each other and not for the scorpions—their prey. The call begins with five rapid throaty sounds, followed by two more that are slower and deeper, and then the last or seventh note is held for many seconds, until it flattens out in silence. A comical call I thought at first, and charming like its name, which I associate with the Spanish verb *besar*—to kiss. This marvelous little reptile has his roof, his mate, and his call—be it his mating call or music of the spheres or a miniature dance of death. And he has his prey—the evil scorpion, which knows not of evil—but even so, this little roof reptile cannot be scorned for his feasting.

His world is in perfect harmony. At least here on the Pacific coast of Mexico, my *besucon* has reached the apex of intelligent adaptability—a magnificent *cold-bloodedness*. His survival means death to the scorpion. Perhaps he is like the executioner who, having effectively resisted evil in the eyes of his peers, can be allowed to commit it. But he is not a symbol for me. If I must kill, I will not dress the part.

    I tell you, I've changed!
    (Laughter.)
No, it's different this time, I mean it!
    (Laughter.)

Who told you the moon was made of cheese or that it was a woman? Look more closely through a telescope—it's stone. Even on full moon nights, its beautiful mask appears remote. Not a word, only a luminous blank stone. A mask which can never be torn off for it covers a face exactly like that of the mask.

    But how does it end?
    The words stopped coming.
    Then it may go on or yet end?
    Or never end.
    Why so difficult?
    The end is the easy part.

I caress my notebook as a lover. I write so hard I can see memory taking shape through the permeable membrane of the fibrous paper.

    Then what are these marked pages, these melancholy passages?
    It's my little estate, and I'm its caretaker.
    But who are you?
    I pursue myself relentlessly...

A Faded Mosaic

My life, my life, now I speak of it as of something over, now as of a joke which still goes on, and it is neither, for at the same time it is over and it goes on, and is there any tense for that?   —Samuel Beckett

I

From a period of reconsideration I consider life in periods—interweaving fugal voices, theme and variations, melting glaciers—at the center when both declared I love you in quotes to signal the cliché.

To make a visual art of words, a music of words resounding as music resounds, yet not an art of declarations, as if there is something to declare. Emphasis leaves its stain of images making an art be: Come images in the beauty of the time it lives in this space of creation. At the beginning of fertility, the belief we shall create always. Message to be read as reader imagines, heard as music, seen as figure or design of thought, in fragments of disintegration in the form of one's idiosyncratic style.

The vision that is and is *not* the vision, being a paradox lost in the eye of the beholder. I must have poetry in a woman or poetry after losing a woman—desires shining in the dark while this old typewriter grins.

When I remember someone harshly I look at the poems of that period even more harshly and those photographs of us—married, but looking like brother and sister, an obvious tip-off.

Last page of borrowed life could not sleep for watching your sleep of pleasurable moanings. In the mornings you remembered nothing—not cat hairs on the pillows, not the clanking coffee pot, not the rain. Startled by thunder you went on sleeping as I soothed remembrance of our patient early years before you would let yourself come, forgetting such warm affection across cold distance.

I was the vicious animal who turned on you when you slammed the door of our cage. You did not know whether to feel "chosen or marked." When our door was locked and chained, I kicked it down. I lost you a long time ago, but I'm not gnawing at this derangement. You set free the deep water in an iron-aged bucket thrown into the abyss—yet you still fear the depth as the bucket slides up an, angry rope, empty but bloodstained. I'm replenished from below as the unconscious thins out, cools into this water I trust.

Systems break down, engines break down. Resistance of a once formally balanced man haunted by infidelities, who will kill to be free of what runs across his face at night. Writing the first word that comes to mind and the next words that come, until the name of names gets mentioned, and he is unmasked.

Our grammar of aloneness matched understanding. I will not think of you so much as you will come to mind. The absurd plays with logic as a pleasure of indirection that logic fails to grasp.

II

I wanted reality to include fantasy, but you wanted love. Neither wanted to kill enough to drag the other's body out. Perhaps the absurd posing as logic trumps aloneness, and passes as a solitary idea. There are questions in these fragments.

Circles within circles are equal, but triangles are not equilateral when geometry lies in its precision, for only the finest lies are precise. Truth *and* consequences corny, yet they crust the heart while gravity laughs.

Viewed from a jet, a miniature barge creates wide arcs in the black Mississippi as you cross, driving toward home—all invisible aspects of this landscape I look down upon, getting lost up here where I was in love with you before the lower case ribbon of sanity broke, drowning in a river that does not flow.

Words move furniture, break hearts in the process. Humiliation seeks its own level to drown, intimacy expensive, talk cheap, priceless suffering of vanity in vain, literature literally littered with last gasps, a body of nakedness in one's own hands.

A version of aversion as acts of love—levels of humiliation where humor lies underlying lies, but what's *under* that? Blue the color of shameless nostalgia, of bitterness wiped clean, but blue cannot be destroyed. Voices melted in scalding water, bloodstains as code, your scent in my beard when I opened wet lips to find you trembling there. I read poems between your thighs, tasting without shame, on page three of a letter unanswered. Still you remain still, face fixed in photographs, first and last names lost pieces of a mosaic written as a memoir.

Gazing from above, she becomes more beautiful as he merely gets more critical. The bizarre becomes commonplace, paranoia of real fear. Ravished by doubt she never recovers from a cruel-but-honest-addiction.

Lady Climax against the wall sighs: "You send me to the other side when we make love, but when you get me in this position you always make a deal I can't refuse." Letting go by refusing her one last royal fuck.

As a participating voyeur he rejects them while they misunderstand him. He paid dues twice but lost both receipts. Too late to imagine a different world in the old or to see the same world in the new. No woman saintly enough to save him—he grieves beyond the allotted time, expecting a generous recommendation.

III

All over but the shouting matches that go on and on after elimination obvious—violent reflex to persuade, despite fact that the shouter listens to an empty echo of victory by shouting, while waves of music ebb and flow on an ocean beneath a sky swallowing stars without a whisper.

"I single out victims in the resonance of pain," she pointed out. "If they're near, they resonate. You do understand the difference, I presume?" she asked, to mock a question. "I must presume a plurality of differences," I replied, to mock an answer. Last time he saw her alive, she was awakened by a nightmare; fearful of hearing those voices he could not hear.

They have withdrawn from the fire, since they held no answers for the flame, could not explicate the smoke, retreating to a safer distance to understand the signal. It was a love he resisted as too needy, unpredictable, mad. A love she denied as too defensive, untouchable, sad. Return to fire, stamp out embers, and push faded questions over a ground of knowledge with a crooked stick, spreading ashes.

There shall be no victimology here. Both gloated over their defeats! Trauma to drama to melodrama. Time to leave when a fine madness becomes a crude one.

Yet when comes that solitary hour without self-defense, of not asking questions of oneself, there is no answer. Only inarticulate responses—her huffy huff and cynical laugh, that desperate snort of ignorance. Merely re-labeling a chemical imbalance alters not the worst effects of suicidal depression or murderous rage.

Who knows when blades fly from suspicion to paranoia? How to defend against what *never* happened?

—What did you mean when you said: *Deserts are oases of neglect*, she asked.

—Threats pale, hateful declarations of love wither with the season.

—And when you said: *Venus is barren in space yet opulent in time*?

—Beauty does not die, only the eyes that behold it.

—And what did you mean by *beautiful suffering blossoms into art*?

—Wounds penetrate, yet the beast survives by tortured logic.

—And when you said: *We can forgive but we cannot forget*?

—Time heals all wounds except the wound of memory.

IV. *Fin—Finis—Finito*

—But it's all merely a performance, no?

—Yes, but based on reality.

—Who is she or who are these three women?

—She has been, and will be, the one and the many.

—The missing piece of the mosaic?

—Yes, she must always be the missing piece.

—Then when may we interview her?

—Never, since she exists only in fantasy.

—Then who's *he*, your narrator and voyeur?

—A poor actor, a spoiled sport.

—And who are you?

—I represent him.

—What do you mean by "represent"?

—I am to be whom he lost.

—And what do you mean by that?

—In this act he has slipped behind the scenery.

—By which you mean backstage?

—Yes, trying on the wardrobe of a dead actor.

—Why?

—A perfect fit.

—What was meant by trauma to drama to melodrama?

—I mean to say he understood every *other* minute of it.

Maximinutiae

Gestures

　　In the beginning—The word. In the reading —Text as bridge. In the crossing—Translation. In the end—Rereading.

Paths Left By Reading

　　Pages are marked in the margins with dashes, brackets, checks, arrows, asterisks, and underlinings made during the first reading. Upon rereading, additional marks are made near other passages, as if those had failed to impress on the first reading, or perhaps were misunderstood earlier. Rereading follows and finds new passages to mark, making the path well worn and leaving footprints in the blissful paradise of a magical text. But it is also a clear sign that one must find a fresh copy of a great book, leaving it unmarked for the next reading.

Crossroads

　　Mid-life crisis determines when—or if—one has enough courage to return to the original path from which one has strayed.

Escapes

We expect poets to make the real fantastic and the fantastic real. When novelists fail to remember they have their characters forget.

Otherness

Inclusiveness may bring the *Other* into a literary canon, but in a society of exclusion the *Other* remains outside the margins, enduring subtler discrimination.

Negative Capability

When I introduce mutual friends who proceed to be critical of this generous host.

Blueprints

To construct a roof: Cut out design in sky, fill pyramid with matter. To make a path? Open the book and begin walking.

Theater or Theatre?

Genesis from Sophocles to Shakespeare to Beckett. Poetry speaks as the first actor; dialogue becomes the second; sculpture in the shape of a woman takes center stage; and our fourth actor will be none other than silence. The gods did not create poetry, poetry created the gods.

Conjugations

Eternal illusion of religious prophecy parallels Romantic delusion of secular freedom. Modern Utopia of creature comfort equals delusions of technological dominance and a false promise of security. Embrace self-conflict in order to transcend it. Short-Circuit: Conclusions drawn upon assumptions made. We cannot conjugate reality.

Asides

Begin with a dose of subjectivity in Realism and a tedious catalogue of objectivity in Naturalism. See a shimmer of reality in Impressionism and a primal slash of life in Expressionism. What was the point of Pointillism again? Out of chronology, we spy a drawing room formula in French Surrealism yet learn the path through wild nature in the modern Spanish-language poets. Triviality in Dada's stepchildren. Reduction to outlines in Minimalism. Eventual erasure: Deconstructionism. All the arts lead to an Abstract Expressionism. Synthesis: Cubism—the square root of art, removing a blindfold from the mind's eye.

Agree or Disagree?

We all agreed on Shakespeare, Mozart, Rembrandt. Certain factions could *not* accept the loss of Sophocles, Beethoven, Klee. Picasso designed a postmodern postcard in hell. Freud and Jung were dispatched from the unconscious to decipher it. We have been trying to explain their explanations ever since. No agreement.

Other Gnomic Tyrannies

The margin and the text. Rhyme and the alphabet. The blank page as space of silence *and* language. Aperture as mirror *and* window. *Other* as prison *and* horizon.

Relativism

Curious that in our time of pervasive relativism, the common reflexive responses are: *Exactly* and *Absolutely*. Yesterday's democracy becomes today's definitive mediocrity. The monkey on our back is not a terrorist, but merely the blind weight of humanity's undeveloped spirituality.

The New Clichés
    There are three sides to every story: Hers, his, and the truth. And there are three sides to every coin: Heads, tails, and the edge. It is neither about the half-full nor half-empty glass, but only about the wine.

Apertures
    Text of openings rarely seen yet always there. Borders do not circumscribe a field of vision, but open to the other side.

Vision
    In the signature of the child—our sense of wonder.

Aesthetics of Waste

Immediate Goals

To put aesthetics back into philosophy.

Second: Debate those who wantonly strip aesthetic limbs from the tree of philosophy due to their petty obsessions.

Third: To remove trash from philosophy and smuggle philosophy into garbage pickup. Finally, to get it out *on time* Mondays, but with variations that may offer some imaginative and entertaining possibilities.

On Arrangement

Arrangement is important. By important I do *not* intend significance. By *is* I mean it is what it is. The period marks the end of the sentence under this subtitle.

On Form

Arrangement does *not* mean form, although an arrangement can take on form, but only after the fact of arranging. Arrangement is the mother of form. Mothers must make arrangements in order to give us form. I do not quest after form, but desire only arrangement. I do not consider form a higher aesthetic term, but merely of no interest here, except perhaps secondarily, when speaking of aesthetics in general.

Is Arrangement Composition?

Not precisely. We can compose music but we can only compost garbage. We can compose ourselves, but we ourselves can only decompose. We *can* can food, even can laughter, but we must *arrange* our garbage.

Garbage and/or Trash?

This debate has attracted the attention of philosophers since antiquity. As Pliny the Elder often exclaimed, "When I think of garbage, I can think of nothing else!" We have been involved right to the present with the debate of accumulation *v.* disposal. Some important philosophical contributions to this question in recent centuries are: Kierkegaard's *Either/Or*, which in Danish translates to *Garbage/Trash*; Heidegger's *Being and Time* literally means *Being* on *Time*; Sartre's *Being and Nothingness* is that long existential lament on the absence of regular collections in occupied France during World War II. All these illustrious tomes bring esoteric philosophy down to street level. That is, garbage juxtaposed so resolutely with trash, enters the blind alley where it will be collected (alas, not in tranquility).

Praxis as Postscript

Unlike these thinkers and Despots of Waste Management, I make no etymological distinction between the terms, because I find these essences exist together in a natural balance of aesthetic coexistence.

Sculpture

In the sense that my "garbage" is three-dimensional, I view it as sculpture—generously and freely arranged, rough or soft in texture, exquisite or tawdry as content, depending on a diverse randomness. This does not preclude the forlornness of bottles—aesthetically *not* ecologically recycled, plus all disposable materials light enough to be lifted by hand.

A Famous Painter and Neighborhood Dogs

Matisse, unaware of my contributions to art, wrote: "One can't live in a house too well kept, a house kept by country aunts. One has to go off into the jungle to find simpler ways which won't stifle the spirit." This is why I randomly arrange socially redeemable objects, like a vacuum cleaner attachment or a perfectly fine lampshade. The blue shade was the crowning glory of last week's work, but unfortunately the sanitation workers did not value it, and it was summarily crushed by the automatic lift. On the other hand, perhaps Matisse's remark might also refer to trash too well kept. Thus I do not attempt to prevent the dogs from taking my careful arrangements to task. In the manner of action painting, they attack with a furious joy.

Found Art?

Nothing is found in garbage or trash for nothing is lost.

Minimalism

"Nothing" is obviously the key word in the last meditation. Minimalism is almost nothing, but not quite lacking enough to be *nothing*. Sometimes I place only the smallest items (an empty milk carton, an old salt shaker, a crumpled cigarette pack) in the simplest minimalist arrangement I can imagine, set down in that brown circular emblem in the green grass.

Beauty

What are aesthetics without beauty? Remember that Romantic pictorial notion of character, as in "that face has character"? This is what an old metal can calls to mind—Character or Beauty in this aesthetic sense. That is, she has a pretty face but she is not beautiful. That is, what an ugly load of garbage, yet beautifully arranged.

Suffering

At first this immense project seemed disgusting. Physically, I handled a combination of chicken bones, coffee grounds, rotting vegetables, and the essence of kitty litter boxes. Intellectually, I thought of canned concepts of waste. Ethically, I realized the political incorrectness of the non-biodegradable nature of the plastic arts. Aesthetically, I saw how utterly ugly were garbage bags and trash sacks of any color—in fact, a sinister sight with aggressively broken bottles protruding. But I had to overcome all these obstacles, knowing that one must suffer for one's art.

Identity

If you saved all your refuse, archeologists might determine a profile of your character, even your identity, just as scholars reconstruct the lives of artists. Face it, you cannot take it with you, so why save it? From this we can derive an important axiom: You are what you dispose.

Waste can be raised to high art, but only if you learn to predispose. I live to dispose. I think, therefore I predispose.

Moderation

Conversely, I am not suggesting that these meditations get out of hand, or become too time-consuming, or take up too much of your intellectual space—rather, the moderate moderation of the Greeks is strongly advised.

Balance

I am reminded of the graceful manner of postmodern sanitation workers, acrobats on the city payroll, who never fall from those swiftly moving trucks.

Window Panes

Sit here. Face the window. Do not stand or relax. Do not tilt your head or blink. Ease into a lasting position. Concentrate. You owe the window a statue.

The window is systematically partitioned into panes by wooden frames, each an episode of serious study.

First pane, bottom left. Two panes to its right, three above each. Elementary. Now notice that a tree seems to divide this pane in half. Do *not* be deceived. You may wonder what lurks behind that tree? Perhaps nothing, since it is an extremely sparse tree. Notice the open door of a delivery truck in the bottom left corner. It appears as only a green smudge at the far left and moves to a window in the door of the truck. Through the truck's window another bare tree, clinging to a few forlorn leaves. There is a sedan across the street, also the rear of a dented station wagon. In the distance, standing on the top stoop of a brownstone, a woman who cannot see you. She is never to move.

Middle pane, bottom row. Automobiles on the other side of the street near a *No Parking* sign. No objects on this side. The restrictions cannot be deciphered from here. An old yellow brick house deposits the first of its three floors in this pane. Bottom right. The tops of those automobiles. Another bare tree, with supports at its base.

Across the street—empty concrete steps. A window on the bottom floor of an old gray brick house. A man, unmoving, peers through that window. He sees your face through the middle pane in the second row of this window. Never desert that pane.

Second row, left. The second and third floors of the brownstone and the yellow brick house. We can see that the yellow paint has been scorched. Windows on the second floor have been boarded up. The fire did not reach the bottom panes. Middle pane, second row. Most of the gray house with its abandoned terrace. Remainder of the gray house is in this right pane, second row. All shades are drawn.

The rooftop of the brownstone is in the third row, left pane. Sky should be bluer, but the pane seems somewhat dusty. This will be remedied immediately. Some scrawls in the dust—perhaps in a foreign script—indecipherable. It fades into the cloud at the extreme left.

Third row, middle pane. Rooftop of red brick house, part of gray house. More sky, slightly bluer. The sky is pierced by a television antenna, not a common antenna, but part of an intricate network. That bird there—completely out of control—drops from the antenna and flies over the gray rooftop and then, appearing as the same bird though you can be assured this is not the case, it leaves a red brick chimney in its wake. Do not concern yourself with these images of birds. This is intended by the enemy to confuse you.

Sky in the top left pane and the brick edge around your studio window. Middle pane, more sky, more edging. Do not twitch, it can never improve your view. Above that is merely more sky. And finally, top right, only sky again. Fine. We have reached the end of our first phase. Now the window will be raised.

You will be allowed to witness the entire view at once. Do not blink. Notice, there was nothing lurking behind the wooden frame. Notice that the woman still stands stiffly obedient. And the man waiting, not blinking. Now take special notice of the bird in the street. It is no longer flying, it does not twitch, it will be in the bottom middle pane once the window is dropped—there, as you see.

Do not be confused by this dead bird. When we think you are ready, it will be removed from that windowpane.

Guards

It was dusk and the visibility was naturally limited. Yet the guards remained transfixed in a circle around the street lamps.

"They're guarding them," Penelope explained. My daughter, seven years and a few feet tall, watches them hypnotically, assured that they have significance, but that it is not immediately known.

"But what for?" I ask.

She smiled. "Daddy, don't you see? It's to keep the others from looting."

"Oh, I see," I assured her, and began watching also.

It appeared they were simply guarding the street lamps, just as she had said. Suspended from each light fixture was a microphone, to which they listened intently. A voice spoke and, each time it did, the lights were extinguished, so that the entire street gone dark intensified the sound of these words: "Do not leave your posts."

All this time strange noises rose from below. They were not leaving their posts, but actually clinging to them, hugging them and emitting brutish grunts.

They were instructed to search in the dark and to "Report all enemy advances in direct ratio to the light loss and in direct proportion to the enemy's body count, color, and shoe size." Then we heard a mass shuffling away from the poles and finally, under the glow of the returning lights, the troops checked their weapons. I say "troops" only because I have no exact reference. They maintained a regimental quality and a military decorum that calls to mind this idea. Plus the similarity of dress, from fatigues down to black boots, and faces with blond moustaches.

Penelope opined, "It's only a practice drill." I tended to agree, because the troops, in addition to their strictness of dress, also wore white Bobbie socks similar to hers, but theirs were somewhat muddy, she informed. Such intuition, this child, or perhaps merely sharper eyesight.

The guarding went on for several days, just after the city had been consumed by fire. For weeks I tried to avoid the problem when I saw it developing, telling my wife that "We should move from this depressed area, trouble is coming." But Agnes was always too depressed to move. So we waited it out, hoping it would pass, until the inevitable happened to our record shop downstairs.

Penelope had put a sign in our window: Mozart Forever. I could have told her it would not work, but Agnes, mutely ironing, would not take my side. The child and her mother have, in very different ways, no sense of cruel chaos. The sign had no positive effect on the looters. They removed what they must have considered the popular albums from our shop and then set fire to it. All the classical and jazz albums melted in a tremendous fury. We were upstairs, trying to prevent the floor from burning through the shop ceiling. We managed to accomplish this by letting the bathtub overflow. But we could not keep

Penelope from screaming in anguish. She wanted to rescue her Mozart.

I suspect that the vigil of guarding will be maintained for at least another week, although the presence of the guards, who casually shot several looters, did not prevent the gutting of our record shop. I suppose this is meant as a "cooling-off period," but the actual cooling off was accomplished by the bath water and the fire department's water hoses. This would be, more consistently speaking, a drying-off period. But even the guards seem to have remained damp from the ordeal.

As a show of hospitality—but also to assure the troop of guards that we were not "enemies" (a loaded word I would never use)—Penelope took them some of our most exquisite, fluffy towels during the drying-off period. But it seems that cruelty (or perhaps police policy) recognizes no bounds. They refused the towels, and dear little Penelope was made to cry.

Novel Bridge

> I will not let myself become tired. I will jump into my story even though it should cut my face to pieces.
> —Franz Kafka

I am writing a novel—
Can do nothing else, want to write something else, anything else; it seems I've been writing this novel throughout life, probably not, too melodramatic, certainly there was a time before the novel, was it only waiting patiently, perhaps it doesn't expect to be finished, or it may not be a novel (is that a question?).

I am trying to write about the past—
It returns slowly, revealing that in youth I organized all the games, games we made physically rough, games that demanded agility, speed, shrewdness.

Perhaps I'm merely playing a game—
While excluded from their games, perhaps they thought I would not play in one they had organized, or they wanted a private, leisurely game, one I would not dominate,

one that despite stacking the odds against myself, I won anyway.

No, I'm writing a novel—
A novel is being written, a novel is writing me, I am a novel. It is insatiable, it sucks up everything, I don't resist it, don't know how to resist it, don't even know its nature, can't see any blood flowing, lungs have not collapsed, yet I feel sucked dry, energy must escape silently through the pores.

The novel keeps me awake—
Perhaps sleep will be the last chapter, I don't know; these are wild speculations from which I wish to walk away, but cannot.

The novel becomes my clothing—
When I try to run away naked it becomes the rain and when I try to go under cover it becomes my skin. If I wanted to kill myself it would become suicide, a mirror laughing in its own face.

If I attempt to leave the studio—
A door opens to another room of the novel where I go walking across an old wooden bridge of childhood, a bridge across the bayou in which snakes swam, but gone now, bridge demolished, bayou dried up.

I remember that bridge—
Where snakes did not seem poisonous, the bayou did not stink, but now I know the old wooden bridge was

dangerous—its oldness, woodness, bridgeness—no, these dangers are too conceptual, the bayou seems hideous now, and snakes were death.

I crossed that novel bridge every day—
Because I had two friends on the other side, I know they must have talked behind my back, I cannot blame them. I was the one who excelled at the things that mattered then as I crossed that bridge to their turf, where perhaps they had organized those games from which I was excluded, they said nothing, there was nothing for them to say, since I was also the fiercest fighter.

Yet the novel hears them—
It has phenomenal hearing that soars above what we think is silence, it could always hear characters talking, their exact words, my novel hears them and this wounded singing, it knows the language of pain.

But what is this novel—
The only game I have played organized by someone else, a miserable character, let me tell you that much, know little else, I learn as I go.

Fragments float by—
I examine them carefully, they stink, my hands are sieves through which the bayou flows, snakes swimming unseen, it takes a novelistic vision for that, they swim under the surface, come up for air in the reeds, the air above so thick and slimy you see only a trail of murky water, snakes slipping by disguised as words.

The novel is a bridge—
Cross if you dare, the wood is rotten, bridge sways, let one foot step in front of the other, your balance is steady in this novel that waits on the other side, resting in the hands of those reading under that tree.

The novel has already been written—
You are a character in it, they will recognize you, as readers of this novel bridge under which the bayou flows— no surprise if you stall for time, since it was written that way. They can wait forever, being as patient as this novel.

A Dream of Footsteps

My father is pitching an old blackish softball, looks like a shine ball, nothing on the ball but age, no tobacco or spit, some sweat maybe, once it had adhesive tape that tore off, everything stuck to the old adhesion, he throws it overhand, a sweet arc, not fast, it's supposed to be hit, no pitchers only servers, right-down-the-middlers, a family game, uncles, cousins, paternal grandpa playing too, using a tiny glove, wearing a silly hat, never played baseball in his life, old now, more than eighty, clowning around, hat turned to one side, my father clowning too.

I'm watching, they won't let me play, never actually say so, I just feel it, I say you know I got better equipment than these old gloves, where did you get this old stuff, who needs new equipment, pops says, still pitching, ball hit right back to him, snags it, laughs, grandpa way out of position, another ball hit, high fly straight out to center, he drops it, the batter gets to third, next pitch a grounder to pops, he scoops, fires home, catcher just standing there, ball hits the wooden backstop, run scores, why didn't he go to first or tag the runner going down the line, could've been the third out. A player saunters over, Louie, a friend from schooldays, his dad died in an industrial accident, he says his mother just committed suicide in the front yard of his sister's house, one shot, they thought it was a backfire, didn't find her for a few hours, she'd given the kids all the money from the accident insurance, they weren't interested in her, except Louie, he was always a good kid, the only one we knew who'd lost both parents, but he couldn't play baseball worth a damn.

    I start walking away from the game, light gets dimmer, reach an excavation site, part of an elevated superhighway to the left, in disrepair, sun descending. I'm walking on a muddy embankment, to the right a barbed-wire fence, over that fence a field of high untamed weeds, reminding of wheat, field almost dark, back to my left a muddy slope down to a ravine under elevated concrete stanchions. Rutting about in the ravine a buffalo with its back turned, intent on muddy water, not drinking, washing rather, looking frustrated in the attempt, it turns my way, thick fur shaggy and wet, eyes directed this way, interested but not suggesting attack, to be safe I climb over the fence, shirt and pants get torn, I get over and stand in the field, buffalo turns away, intent on watering again, thrashing, then he disappears. I look from the west, sky washed orange and crimson, look back due east, completely dark overhead, no stars, a suggestion of light in the grass, moonlight but no moon visible, sun gone down, going down seemed routine yet it's suddenly dark.

    I walk across the field, turning I see a shadow over my right shoulder, shadow of a man on the other side of the fence, a small man, his stature reminds of grandpa, too dark to see his expression, yet I know it, expression neither cheerful nor mournful nor any other adjective except perhaps disinterested, unsettling nonetheless. I move away from that shadow, deeper into the weeds, hiding, completely covered by a web of foliage, I know he's climbed over the fence in pursuit, not menacingly, I feel no fear only irritation, he taps me on the shoulder, I don't look at his face, looking back over the shoulder he's tapped, I know I will see only what I've seen before, an old man, small of stature, looking at me.

    I run, it's not difficult running on level ground, weeds not tangled, but no space to sprint, from a distance the field seems thick but the height of the weeds hides the openness within, then it turns marshy, no footing yet, I run faster, he never loses a step, can't hear his steps but know he chases, I reach the concrete of an open parking lot, streetlights, row of houses, three dogs run away from us, footsteps on the concrete, first sound I hear, they aren't his footsteps, the houses disappear, run into an alley, narrow high walls, no light, a chain link fence in the distance, it glistens, yet he's right behind me. I pull up at the fence, dead end, I turn to fight, he's old and gnarled, I pick him up by his old coat at the shoulders, a baggy coat easy to grab, I throw him against the fence, his collar catches on the X pickets atop it, he tilts down like a scarecrow, smiling now, body limp, arms dangling, baggy pants, laces untied.

    I leave him, run back up the alley to the street, across the parking lot, moon out full now, see clouds above the luminous field, I won't return there, turn away, running in an endless rectangular shadow, the light in the field blazing, I run faster, moon gone behind the clouds, no light, no sound except footsteps.

Bagatelles

On Motives
>—What was his motive for murder?
>—A raging hatred.
>—What caused his reaction?
>—She slept with another man.
>—Why this reason?
>—She offered no other.
>—Did he desire a particular motive?
>—Apparently not.
>—Why?
>—He was impatient.

On Problems
>—Isn't death a knotty problem?
>—What do you mean by knotty?
>—Like a knot, in the sense that we are bound by it.
>—No, life is the knot. Death unties it.

On Puns
>—Is your philosophy composed entirely of puns?
>—Not entirely.
>—Could such a philosophy be profound?

—It might be amusing.
—What would obviate its profundity?
—Over-intentionality.
—Are your puns always intended?
—Only when developed from a play on words.
—Is that the secret of their popularity?
—The original pun was benign.
—Another cliché?
—The pun is a metaphor without conscience.

On Method Acting
1. For wound or illusion, apply a soiled bandage.
2. Wrap it tightly and do *not* remove.
3. Encourage infection.

Twilight Texts

Fragments

    To understand fragments in a sequence as a valid perspective of one overwhelming experience. To see facets of a prism unknown by one vantage or from another point of view, since angles change and viewpoints evolve. Not absolute repetitions in time but timeless variations.

How to Experience "Experience"

    According to this computer, "experience" is a repeated word in this text. Technology seems unable to grasp the concept of experience as variation. One lover often repeated that I kept "a deep dark secret," meaning evil rather than intriguing. An old friend's immediate retort upon hearing of her haughty claim: "No doubt darker than deep." Hearty laughter tumbled after this wit—a deeper way to *experience* experience. To experience a mentor's example as a text moving toward art but never reaching that horizon. The art of living in revisions. Yet to encounter lucid minds with beautiful souls, or to perceive a naked face of genius at a glance, is to know it intuitively by first utterance!

Aesthetic Imperfections

Kafka—on the other side—fixates on a chaste *verminization* of the body. Behold brothers in a crumbling pantheon, a burning map and a boot of blood, polar opposites in their quest, while vulnerable language writes across the vast middle. Considering that external arrangements must be projected from internal rooms, the slightest adjustment of this lampshade can be moved by a subtle shading of thought, while the desk's mass reaches into an impulse of the lower back to straighten the spine when intention finds form. The absurd plays with logic from twilight analysis to midnight paralysis, while each time we plagiarize a mirror, the typewriter clucks against silence, grinning with black plastic teeth.

Multiple Choice

What's the sound of one hand clapping?

A. Eternity's tapping on the jagged tooth of time.

B. Echo of the Master's hand against the face of a novice.

C. Meister Ego vigorously patting himself on the back.

Meister Ego

Pomposity my albatross, touts Meister Ego in a devious tone, inflated with a fame of lurid origin, cribbing a *Thesaurus*. Manic pursuit of hunter tracing hysterical flights of prey. Who would assassinate the last word except in fear of The Great Silence? Ponder twilight's joy—infinite space without objects. Forcing extremes just to write about it becomes a tedious obsession. Guilt assumes autonomous existence, shedding rare tears at absurd events. The too-self-conscious-text on the consciousness of self forges a separate world no one can inhabit. Death exhibits all its banal symbols. I give up, I go on. I doubt I believe. I fear I'm courageous. I run the narrow, swim the wide. Avoid ceremonies and swallow my bride. Cross a bridge as I build it, create a genius child without a mother. Bury a seed in a garden, refusing domestication by a puzzle in which I will not fit. Being too wild a piece.

An Amateur's Guide to the Arts

Listening with passionate enthusiasm to classical music and jazz creates the fantasy that we can compose, improvise, and master any instrument. Reading poetry with the same passion creates the illusion we can compose new literary forms, reinvent language, and project any voice imaginable. Music and poetry emerge from our silent anticipation yet both return to that critical silence beyond our mastery.

Survival

I sing the survival of instants, the next word, shifting light. Existence an accidental conceit—we survive the accident, but get buried by theories. Eye reinvents beauty in art, listens to music dance, touches taste. Scent a silent wonder as we ripen or rot.

Unnecessary Events

    Another knock at the door.
    Another fictional mistress.
    Another place of exile.
    Another cat to bury.
    Another newscast.

Another Muse.
Another loss.
Another list.

Spiritual Questions

Becoming is connected to solitude's silent encounter with Being. Yet how to speak of the soul? A relic from The Ancient Age of the Holy Ghost? Or lost in Institutionalized Religion *and* Organized Spirituality? Such zeal in chatter of Dead-Again-Christians! Bliss or self-righteousness in Dante's *Paradiso*? Luther's sanctimonious guilt and punishment are stifling. Yet Bach's music never stifles. Being spirit we return to spirit.

Listening to Billie Holiday

Billie cleanses the pallet and conscience as geniuses do. She is a sublime instrument of grief, transforming banal lyrics into poetry. I heard about Billie first from my father and then on my own, for everyone has their own Billie—starting with tenor sax man Lester Young, down to the rest of us. "You wouldn't know it, but buddy I'm a kind of a poet," she sings, and we know her truth.

Abandonment

To be a speck in that desert sky, an image only, fluidly created to contemplate the beauty of grace in her moment. Any utterance about *a Movement* or *the New* will be marginal tomorrow. Name it and it disappears, even as its stereotypes are perpetuated and its clichés are crowned in the literary pages. The contrived text carves a perfect artifice for Ego. The composed text finds its balance in an evolving culture. The open text is a perpetual flow of energy, continuous transformation, much ado about nothingness. The unspoken word is instinct returning to silence, the naming word a codified knowledge, the metaphor an intuition of poetry. Poetry is the transcendent root. Never abandon her.

Incarnations Over Time: Rereading Guy Davenport

First a reader becomes a writer then a translator becomes a poet. Poetry made of light not dust. A poet of pure spirit disguised in elegant prose. A genius leaving fingerprints in revisions. Mist unfurling exotic in the figured leaf, innocence forgiven in crimes of passion. Beauty draws us to the edge of perfection, while our fragile edge struggles against its opposite. Joy in balance, in balancing joy.

Acceptance Speech

I began writing my acceptance speech even though I had not been awarded a prize—simply to be prepared. I submitted to the whims of editors, publishers, agents, and publicists—yet remain unpublished. But I decided that I would rather be a sacrificial lamb than a questioning goat in a nation of sheep, while fleecing every mixed metaphor or available pun. Then again, as the saying goes, should be *now* again.

I was prepared for any jargon about bearing witness or doing lunch. I drafted this speech of acceptance—with a flexible blank to accommodate the name of the award, the prize amount, and a long list of those to thank—since they keep announcing these endless new "genius" winners in a world of countless awards. *Award Winning Author* applies to just about everyone except yours truly. Thus I was prepared when they asked for humble introductions for my betters.

But then another was persuaded to introduce them and I was assigned to introduce *him*, although he needed no introduction, since he more famous than the prize-winner. I sat in the first row as insurance in case of the introducer's absence or sudden heart attack, but lost my seat to a younger, more competitive failed author, while preparing this very text *about* my acceptance speech. (This speech has since undergone revisions, but is not for publication.)

Surprise Coda
Sent a copy of this book as a surprise gift to friends. In melodrama one always must include the pronoun *me* in every text. Also notice the phony sense of self-importance in selecting one's own readers. But who finds oneself in this company? Are they the most perceptive readers known to the writer or are they his *only* friends? Notice, he does not say how many friends. Has he even been truthful about the number of copies he seems to be dispensing? This *Coda* is out of balance with the texts it fails to codify. I take the texts seriously, but I am too self-conscious to send them without the counter weight of humor. That is, I do not take myself so seriously as to think I have something profound to say. Caught in a philosophical tone of cribbed maxims or minimal epiphanies. Or, both are tainted by dishonesty, perhaps intentionally? Never counted words until I had a computer. I suspect that you are *not* surprised by this *Coda*. But I was merely trying to awaken my notebook by

surprising myself. Ego reigns as a necessary mode of daily existence, perhaps, but with inflationary devices that claim consciousness to be a metaphor for art. But the space of solitude must be immersed in underworld depths, leaving the body as an image that searches out the psyche in Hades.

Film Script Never Seen

A man climbs upon a stool but the pyramid of type is too tall. A plant flourishes in the garbage disposal. Cut it, the director commands. A man tumbles from the stool, another plant stretches across the floor. The typewriter types only what the typist keyboards. All fingers point toward: The End.

Clarifying Essential Vocabulary

An alphabetical coincidence or absurd accident has placed the word *sad* between *sacrosanct* and *saddle* in the dictionary. Sacrosanct suggests: Holy, consecrated, sacred; a sanctuary for the rising spirit; a shaping of self selflessly in the service of an ideal. The poet awakened from a nightmare scavenging for his notebook, like an avenging god cries out for blood. But after sipping wine for hours, he wept once more for the sacredness of the poor.

Sad is characterized by sorrow, affected by irreparable loss; feeling miserable or wretched; desolate or in a deep depression. All indicate subtle distinctions for levels of descent, which means *nothing* to the sinking spirit. The retired academic existentialist fell into his bluest despair when he spied the absence of his favorite word *ennui* not among the synonyms for sadness. But after several shots of *cognac*, he enjoyed a dark mood free of vocabulary. This punster made the mistake of fixating on the word *saddle* only to read *sad* imbedded in its leather binding. He did not drink a drop, but pointed out the *parable* hidden in *irreparable* and the *holy* ending of *melancholy*. Alas, misery loves company, but hates the company it keeps.

Forgotten Dialogue

    If my three-dimensional figure casts a shadow, what figure casts me?

    Light, because everywhere at once—

    What one-dimensional shadow does a two-dimensional shadow cast?

    Darkness, except you cannot see it hiding under your shadow.

    And what does this darkness cast?

    It buries itself in the earth—

    And the earth?

    It shines with a blue incandescence—

    And what's this metaphorical light?

    A reflection of memory—

    And where's this reflection now?

    Lost in the light.

Howling at the Moon

Few people have the imagination for reality.
—Johann Wolfgang von Goethe

If I but had the theme on paper—worked out, of course. It is too silly that we have got to hatch out our work in a room.   —Wolfgang Amadeus Mozart

For Mozart I shall write at night and shall account it reading Dante's *Inferno*.   —Lorenzo Da Ponte, Librettist

The Idea of Coffee

I brew enormous amounts of coffee, prepare several cups with milk and honey, but drink only the first cup. I take it down in several hearty gulps—it steams, it burns. I love that first cup of coffee in a way that's indescribable. Yet there might be a way to describe it, positively credible ways with lovely lyrical turns of phrase, but I shall not attempt it.

Suffice it to say all the other cups of coffee matter not. They are virtually untouched. Oh, I sip at them, but only in the inertia created by the excitement of that first cup. I am not a true coffee drinker, for they drink it black only, cup after cup, *a continuo*.

I love coffee not so much unto itself, but the idea of coffee. The ritual of brewing, its measures and perks, its aromas and rising heat, the rich colors of a dark vision, and that first steamy gulp! No doubt if such a savory poison were invented, I would brew it also, and just as lovingly, if only once.

I have been writing every night recently, and the new work is nearly composed. I continue to use pencils, it goes more slowly this way, but how I love the sturdy elegance of a perfectly sharpened pencil, its sensitive adjustment to my grip, as the point slowly disappears.

I write exclusively at night. I never sharpen pencils as I work but choose a new one from a plentiful supply at the ready. And the same with the paper—stacks of blue-lined composition stock, the inexpensive sort used by students. I consider myself a student.

I work under a florescent lamp, a low bar of light above the desk, not as Romantic or as irresponsible as a candle, but steady light is what I need. The lamp's current makes a sound reminiscent of desert insects, a remote buzzing, musically muted, curiously comforting. Yet it might be that I am merely accustomed to the sound, since often and always late, it is the only sound I hear when the pencils are at rest.

I deem a sense of waste the most essential aesthetic orientation the artist must develop. It matters not the modesty of excess, as in my case. I walk to the village every week for a supply of coffee, writing materials, and the little food I eat. Barely can I afford what I use, much less what I waste. Yet I insist on all of it, even when it means I must cut my rations in half. Food has never really interested me, and I eat nearly nothing.

This morning I sharpened forty pencils. Tonight I have used four. At times—I have no idea why and never bother to examine it—I break a pencil, sometimes viciously, although I am never remorseful about it. I have never broken more than three in any month, never more than one during a night's work. It does not constitute a problem since they break cleanly. The few slivers of wood and lead blend in with the dust on the floor, helping to sustain its dry pungency, adding to its distinctive aging. When I broke a pencil tonight, I was thinking of what she had said long ago. I almost broke it a second time—not so easy as one might think—but I have never broken one twice, even when remembering her words.

Today I stacked two hundred sheets of paper for the week's work. I put aside my customary sheets for tonight, but have not filled them. There are six cups of coffee—one empty, five others in a row, untouched. Milk curdled, cups cold. If I had wanted one more cup I would have had to wash one, which I never do at night. Perhaps I need a seventh cup?

How cold it has been tonight. Only my left elbow remains comfortable under the lamp, it warms precisely the area of an old injury, my withered left arm. I am so accustomed to it, I forget it looks differently from the right arm. Fortunately I am right handed. This old lamp has advantages I had not realized when I first bought it at auction for a mere dollar. It has become an elbow warmer, as well as a light source, thus the value of this magic lamp proves to be much greater than its price.

This night is nearly done. I need no clock to know, for my scribbling has ceased. I am staring, my stare is menacing, no one can stare me down, I despise being stared at, I always stare down anyone who dares to stare at me, my stare remains riveted on the bare wall. I imagine myself as a tuning fork for the music of desert insects, overwhelmed to the point of utter agitation and carried away from myself. I know then to fly into the cleaning of coffee cups and spoons.

Nearly dawn and time to rest. I lie on my back, gaze upward at the dark ceiling, it seems to be the most philosophical position, often I pass many morning hours in this very spot. It was not always this way, not when I was with her and not during my youth. Then I slept nights, slept deeply, but not now. I turn on my side, either side, resting when I feel most ambiguous. Suddenly I turn on my stomach, I grunt, I thrash, I rut without thought in this animal position, until the forgetfulness of sleep.

I awaken, brew a fresh pot of coffee, and nod knowingly. I look at last night's work, twelve pages done, two pencils dulled, one broken, and this one with a few remaining degrees of lead, clutched in my hand that veers toward the bottom of this page. With both hands I break the pencil in half. The two pieces are jagged, quite rare, and I find this mildly disturbing. I put the two pieces aside on the desk.

I take up a newly sharpened pencil, which seems so finely tuned I should be able to drive it right through the desk. I have it firmly in hand, set it to a fresh sheet of stock, continuing this life's work on the first line, almost without pause.

Philosophical Reflections

My view of life is meaningless. I suppose an evil spirit has set a pair of spectacles upon my nose of which one lens is a tremendously powerful magnifying glass, the other an equally powerful reducing glass.
—Soren Kierkegaard

I find the letter K offensive, almost disgusting, and yet I use it; it must be very characteristic of me.
—Franz Kafka

What is a poet? Frankly, the most misunderstood of beings. Please ponder the curious paradox of my own case. I have consistently incorporated the most absurd fantasies into my work, only to have them ascribed to autobiography. No one questions the imaginative resources of these fantasies or their philosophical implications—ah no, they beg for more details. Either this has been the case or, when relating an actual experience, the basic validity of my utterance has been doubted. What could be the remedy? Must I begin lying to everyone I see face-to-face, or deviously weave the real facts into the fabric of the imaginative work in order to be believed?

Most memories of childhood belong to our parents. I've seen the pictures in the family album, but cannot recall appearing in them. As a boy I would dash from the house, I wouldn't slam the door, didn't slam doors in those days, and I'd jog for miles, jogged while conjugating verbs. Later I ran cross-country races on our high school track team, I had speed and endurance. Older I walked, it was a brisk pace mind you, I couldn't resist slowing down, slowing down I couldn't resist peering into lit windows at night, can't resist yet, difficult to talk about it, talking sends sentences running on into the night, no effort was considered too rigorous in order to see inside those windows, containing scenes that were usually mundane, but I remained detached, transfiguring everything, making life extraordinarily rich. A voyeur leads two lives.

Taboo creates excitement, as too much stultifies desire. Excitement from defying taboos presents the possibility of delicious punishment, which is usually administered. Primal fear waiting forever in dread of ecstasy!

How is it that opposites are supposed to attract? I go bouncing off every thing and every one. I suspect my body and soul are double negatives.

Knowing what we know to be infinitesimal, we can never know all we don't know, although we can guess it to be infinite. Knowing this, there's at least the knowledge that in hoping to know more there's no real hope. Never knowing real hope could also mean that there's no hope at all. And without hope we cannot go on. Yet knowing so little, we have no choice.

The mirror reflects an honest image but other images lie. The mirror sees the eyes growing older, sees that squinting has brought wrinkles and lines forward. I don't fear aging, for the older the eyes the more beautiful they become—seduction moves up from the mouth, the poor mouth that can only withdraw with age, having tasted and regretted. Yet the eyes still watch, seeing wrinkles as memories of passion.

Following a blind man along the sidewalk, I realized the impossibility of writing a poem about him. It was too late for the idea of blindness to be perceived as other than symbolic blindness. Yet there was this blind man, I could see him, I followed him along an unfamiliar sidewalk; he might have led me anywhere. We stopped. We were at the corner, he was listening for the traffic to halt, our encounter was brief, it consisted of two words: Go on. He turned, smiled, nodded, turned, and went on. I stood at the corner, watched him cross the intersection, observing a man who truly played life by ear. I stepped into the street—a horn blared—I jumped back.

Each dawn I stare out the same window. Perhaps I should wash the window since I must open it to see anything at all, but this morning the window stuck. Why wash it, why not watch the distortion that filthy panes offer? How simple without all that strenuous nonsense of washing or trying to open it, how marvelous to ponder shadowy light in its shattering maze of abstraction.

Through the bathroom exhaust fan I can leisurely hear her monotonous tooth brushing soliloquies that at first were exotic. The aural registers a richer experience than the visual. I listen but never seduce, for the voyeur is the epitome of pure desire.

Infants seem to be speaking English when they say "da-da"—but they're speaking their own language. When we hear infants speak in a foreign tongue, we're even more remote from comprehension. However when these two infants are placed in a crib together, they seem to understand each other perfectly.

Does the patient resent the analyst's petty authority because the analyst ignores the profound authority of the irrational? They'll not only attempt to drive you insane, they'll succeed efficiently, you'll be kept in constant touch with your deterioration, it's the manner they love, everything will be made to appear fair, you'll be told what's happening, made aware that what they've told you has been true, it's this awareness of going insane that actually drives you insane, but this awareness is an illusion that deteriorates in perfect unison with your overall deterioration. In only one instance does this technique *not* work—when you realize that you're already insane.

The ethical life is dull weather, its forecasts are drawn up like marriage parchments: *Till death do us part.* If the Medieval Romance called Marriage continues, the escape hatch of divorce must be less expedient. When a couple separates, their parchment should be submerged in a slow acid that will consume the document within one year. If the couple decides to rejoin within that period, each partner must place a hand into the acid, retrieving that portion of the parchment not yet devoured.

Philosophies are empty shells discarded on the shore. We hold them up in admiration. Not for what they say but for how they echo the sea.

Descartes will be remembered always for the process of doubt leading to his *Cogito*. That's not what I remember. Rather it's his assigning letters to known and unknown quantities—earlier letters designating the known, later the unknown. *Ergo*, I chose my name. The letter K is carefree, sporting a strong backbone while thrusting an arm into the air, a foot toward the path. Dust kicks up as K moves *poco moto* down unmarked paths. Life must be *fugato,* possessing the richness of variation a fugue possesses, but without the responsibilities of composition. I think therefore I contradict. Some passages are neither written to remember nor written to forget, but written only to keep one engaged in the act of writing.

Intrigued by Darwin's notion that music is the highest developed form of the sexual cries of animals, I consider the long melancholy song of the humpback whale through oceanic channels of such acoustical qualities that its siren song travels incredible distances, sometimes as far as a thousand miles.

Once I had an idea for a story of a man with extra-sensory hearing, who warns the great city of the coming danger that he alone can hear. Of course they do *not* believe him and cut off his ears in the cruel bargain. Total destruction soon follows. A man will resort to desperate measures in order to be believed. How absurd that these very measures close the case against belief.

Anecdote: Lovers who go through ridiculous machinations to keep their adultery secret only to be discovered when they accidentally meet in the bank.

The wife seems to be deeply attracted to what is predictable in her husband, but she loves him because he's sometimes unpredictable. The mistress, however, being herself unpredictable, loves only his steady manner.

Rules, there are countless rules, the first rule being that every rule has an exception, this never used to be the first rule, now it rules supreme, it negates all the tedious rules that follow. "You will do this," yells the father, considering his utterance a divination, while the mother considers it a domestic command. But a certain child considers it not, knowing it to be nothing more than an exaggerated wish fulfillment.

If once you begin to worry about being lonely in your old age and it turns out to be the case, you will have denied yourself at least one memory of youth to warm you. The more you worry, the more of your life gets spent in advance without interest. Besides, there's no assurance you will reach old age anyway, but only that you will die, which always should be an amusing subject for contemplation.

Absolute honesty toward oneself means facing suicide. Clumsily the bread knife slips back into the drawer. But if contemplating suicide, where should one leave a note? Will they look in the suicide's pocket? Might the note blow off the table or go out with the trash? If they find it, will the handwriting be legible, its message comprehensible? Exactly what should one say and in what tone? Which tense would be proper, present or past? Would a typed note be insincere?

I would never have ended it all, since most of it had already ended. I would simply have ended what remained. Yes, a final confession, the ultimate honorific performance. Please don't be frightened. To frighten someone is worse than being frightened, for in that instant we see the fear of death on another's face.

I almost chose to call myself X, the classical unknown, that unhappiest of men. But I did not chose X, for he's always at a crossroads, deep in self-contradiction, destined to be alone. For X there's never final rest.

Finally tonight I forced open the filthy window. Completely dark outside, except for glinting crystals of snow. Looking back into the room, I distinguished no objects while feeling my way back toward the bed. I sensed a romanticized attitude of blindness until I saw contours and then the cluttered dresser. I sat on the bed, fully dressed, and in those few minutes it became unbearably cold. I slipped off my shoes, shed all clothes, burrowed under the covers. I stared at the window, a dark blue patch at the end of a nearly black corridor. I stared until my eyes closed and I slept.

But during the night I sat up quickly in bed. What was it? I looked around the room, adjusting, as a frigid wind blew through the window. The blue patch was paler, room less dark or eyes more alert, the cold forgotten, nothing else. I leaned forward in the bed, breathed deeply, and then I felt my heart flutter. I was fascinated with the simple exactness of the verb. It wasn't beating or thumping—no it was fluttering, nothing else evokes the sensation. It was that simple: My heart had fluttered like a heart.

The Musical Erotic

Life must be lived forward, but understood backwards. —Soren Kierkegaard

You know that I am, so to speak, immersed in music, that I am busy with it all day—speculating, studying, considering. —Wolfgang Amadeus Mozart

Accidentals

Most abruptly I halted my study of the piano, I'd broken my arm, it never healed correctly, when it hurt for several months the doctor said to be patient, when it hadn't stopped hurting for several years he suggested that I be philosophical. It still hurts, so he suggested we break it again. Who are *we*? It didn't take the plural to break it the first time, but it would take more than a plurality, more than a majority to break it now. Even a unanimous verdict wouldn't do, for it wouldn't be unanimous. Thus my left arm is faulty, a bit crooked, I can't play. Oh, I plunk the keys now and then, only Beethoven's *Für Elise*, well just the first nine notes of it, the notes are: E, D#, E, D#, E, B, D, C, A, nine keys I should've said, not notes, only six notes, six separate notes, all played with the first two fingers of the right hand.

Yes, that's right but let's see which are the first two fingers, they're not called fingers medically, I guess I mean the index digit and the one next to it, that's the middle digit if you count the thumb, it's the longest one if your digits are of normal length, if you watched me play you'd know immediately. With these two little digits I play expertly, I play these nine notes as fluidly as any pianist could play them, I play them perfectly—but alas there can be no concert, no, not even a recital for such humble genius and its display of diminutive brilliance. Alas, I seek no pity, I was no prodigy, and I don't consider the accident tragic, I read music poorly, never played scales well, wasn't even considered a promising student. I played just one piece, played it *poco moto*, my designation for everything, even my sentences—slow, carefree, with a pinch of animation.

My paternal grandfather was an accomplished violinist, he studied in Italy, he wasn't *that* accomplished, he was born there, migrated to America, went to work, got married, wife begot a son, their only child became my father, my father never learned to read music, I never learned why, grandfather tried to teach him but father refused, he ran out of grandfather's house, out the front door as legend has it, he didn't slam it, you didn't slam doors or legends in those days, he ran into the streets without formal musical training. He learned to play his snare drum at large, playing it by ear.

Grandfather wanted father to be a musician, he beat him regularly, they never got along well, father never wanted to be a musician, he never beat me, we got along fine, my father never forgave his father for the beatings, he always ran from the house crying, classical music made him cry, grandfather's violin made him cry, never saw that violin, never saw my father cry, this all part of the legend, it goes on, I never cry, I never ran from my father's house, that's *not* how I broke my arm, if this sentence had a door I'd slam it, if it had a window I'd climb through it, if only it had but it doesn't, if only, no if never, so I end period.

Mozart and I were pianists, relatively speaking, but you can see the difference, both subjects are balanced perfectly by the conjunction, they shouldn't be, not by any laws of logic or music but they are, that's grammar for you—there are pianists and pianists, Mozart broke all the records for genius, I merely broke my arm.

I didn't break it playing piano, I didn't play that vigorously, I didn't cry when I broke it, I almost never cried, the broken arm embarrassed more than expected, much more because I hadn't expected to be embarrassed, at least it didn't ruin my career, I had no career, still it embarrassed me, but not to tears.

Was Mozart assassinated? Either he was *not* assassinated or certain earthly angels, against all known evidence, are susceptible to poison. How else could he have died so young? Kierkegaard loved Mozart, he was like a teenage girl in love with the supreme genius, he admitted this, and he was shameless about it.

Kierkegaard collapsed on the cobblestones of Copenhagen, one of his familiar alleys, he was only forty-two. Mozart died shortly before his thirty-sixth birthday. They both went to Heaven, even though I don't believe in Heaven.

Mozart composed *Don Juan*, his most famous opera, Kierkegaard insisted it wasn't just a classic but *The*

Supreme Classic, no one could argue with him about this question, he didn't consider it a question, for Kierkegaard it was a fact, he had every possible argument to prove his case, all were eventually convinced, even those who couldn't be convinced by logic were seduced by his passionate belief, he was entirely too brilliant, too tenacious about his love-object Mozart, it was only a matter of time when everyone ceased to resist, and finally sighing, "Yes, you are right."

I love Kierkegaard, Kierkegaard loved Mozart, you can see the difference, alas no difference, just the tense, I love, Kierkegaard loved, I live, Kierkegaard died, a matter of circumstances only, yet I don't love Mozart. I don't dislike Mozart, just don't like opera, never attended one, I realize I have no evidence to argue, perhaps I won't go because I refuse to wear a tie, that's not the reason, perhaps I'm slightly envious of Don Juan, the character not the opera I mean, I've never heard the opera, it's the character who interests me, he's received so much attention, he didn't go to Heaven, he didn't go to the devil either, what the hell, he probably never existed, if he did he didn't give all that content to all those forms, Don Juan expired from a life of constant copulation, to die otherwise could only be less interesting, but since I'm of the lower classes, I'm not witty *only* lewd, so I say the Don screwed himself to death.

Have I misled you or have you misfollowed, I was being cautious earlier, I used the capital H for Heaven, don't think *Don Juan* is the supreme classic, don't believe heaven is the supreme classic, perhaps they're imitative fallacies, we know the Don went up in flames, he was not a devil, I don't believe in hell either, don't believe Mozart was an angel, for how could he compose *Don Juan* and be an angel at the same time, angels aren't that versatile.

Versatility seems not my style either, I don't know the Don's techniques, I'm just a lower class poet, can't rhyme or scan, can't even step, neither right foot nor left, both off wrong, should the expression be got off on the wrong step, not bad, there's a little versatility for you, okay *very* little, I'm not the prodigy here, I'm not supposed to fly or leap, just amble *poco moto* with a pinch of animation, usually graceful on my feet, I take my steps now, alas quibbling steps, let's not quibble, I know steps aren't infinite but they're longer than feet, two or one, sometimes none, don't want to discuss *nothingness*, it leaves so little to say and so much space in which to say it.

Mozart flew, I mean he soared, he was a kind of bird perhaps, one of a kind, a rare bird, I can't tell you what kind, he was *that* rare, but he wasn't an angel, he sang, I know angels are supposed to sing even if we can't hear them, Mozart's opera sings, I should buy a record, don't need a tie for that, what a stroke of genius. I can imagine a bird called Amadeus, a delicate bird, a bird who depends on the seeds of his patrons, alas some birds are poisoned, we don't know if Mozart was poisoned, we know he was ill, we know he had rivals, just don't know if Salieri did it.

Either one of his rivals was an assassin or not, if he was it's surely assassination, if not it could have been character assassination, how can character be assassinated, a novelist could knock him off, that's not what it means I don't think, I don't believe in double negatives, perhaps character assassination was only a *rococo* frill like snuff, snuff couldn't kill a character unless he died from sneezing, unless he was snuffed out, but that's not how Mozart died, if he was poisoned by envy, it was poison envy.

Mozart soared but didn't live to be thirty-six. Kierkegaard leaped in faith but died at forty-two. I still stand, yet I'm at a standstill. Perhaps I will live forever, you don't have to be a genius to die young, and already I'm too old to die young.

A Cassandra Variation

How did I break my arm? A fair question, I know a fair question when I hear one, I ought to know, I just asked it. I think it deserves an answer, I'd like to give you one, it's not so simple, there are many, each story has several versions and each version various interpretations and each interpretation seems to be highly conflicting, but all are mine. Here's one version interpreted perhaps to the point of legend, it's the most oft repeated, I don't recall how it manifested itself, but legends do manifest and are oft repeated, although oft should be used if e'er.

Stories are simpler, they get told not manifested, this one's about breaking my arm while trying to compose a fugue at the piano, it's simple but its syntax is not, couldn't compose the fugue with one hand, I was *klavierstück*, I was in pain, all the stories hurt, all variations on the same painful theme, the theme and the subject of these fugal notes, perhaps you thought Mozart or Kierkegaard or Don Juan were my subjects, possibly you might've even been so foolish as to think I was my own subject, a broken subject at that, subject to many interpretations, subject to a crooked object, my love objects, object of many sneers, subject of many lies, my left arm and it's limitations, it defines me, it's my high point, it rests above my head, I need a rest, all music needs rests, I rest my cast.

If not how, then why? I'd like to tell you, it's not so simple either, or it's more complex than how, thinking about it gives me this shrinking desire, I had this desire for her that shrank, did she ask questions, not really, this isn't why, I don't know how, it just happened, but that's another subject, in fact my counter-subject to this fugue, her name was Cassandra, still is, some things can be depended upon, Cassandra could, how did she get in here, didn't expect her in here, under here, why I ask, why is for children to ask, adults must be accepting, more composed.

I wanted to be composed, I wanted to compose, I wanted to compose myself with her, she's more dependable than I recall, memory doesn't perform well, I no longer perform, I no longer have a piano or Cassandra, make nothing of that, I should scratch all this out, I can't, it's like the judge telling a jury to ignore that last remark, it can't be ignored, it can't be stricken from the record, I haven't stricken anything except myself, I'm no judge, here's my complete testimony, it's full of exaggerations, my life is an exaggeration, but for once I'm not exaggerating. Perhaps I should get to the point, there is no point, don't point at me, you're no jury, I won't be accused, it's not my fault, I take things as they come, I'm accepting, adult, composed, I play life by ear, *poco moto*, it's my style, I can't change it.

I don't know what or how or why, can't defend myself, I follow no rules, I simply continue, it's my only rule, it breaks all other rules in time, that's the point, to keep in time, to let the music play, don't ask why the judge judges, how the jury decides, what the grammarian allows, you're lost anyway, you've lost your way, you're a fugue of your own making, forget those scales, scales itch, no scratching, don't alter a note, don't revise a word, don't change, just go on, this is our musical erotic, but I need another comma to hang on to, one more please, there, I go on, and on, yes, and what a relief when that itching under the cast ceases.

In the story it's dark, I stepped forward, feet got crossed, I was listening to fugues for organ on the radio, I stumbled, I fell, falling I thought I had a theory that organ music sounded like death, I dropped the idea when my left arm struck a bedpost, they all said it could've been worse, I should've been joyful, if I'd broken the right they would've said the same, how lucky you did not break both arms, quite right, just the left, that was enough, it hurt like hell, I almost cried, I didn't, it went numb, just in time, I was thinking of death, I vowed to understand it, I vowed stupid things in crises, I devised my theory, a splint would've been better, I fell, or had I fallen, no time to be tense, I struggled, sat up, kneeled, reached the light switch, I could see as the fugue continued. I phoned Cassandra, she called the ambulance, I fainted, woke up in a hospital, was I delirious, do you know if you're delirious when you're delirious, I don't know *being delirious*, but you could look it up. Perhaps I was merely dreaming, a delirious dream, I was with Cassandra, we were in her father's pickup, is that one or two words, but dreams don't stop to spell, it was a green truck, that made me think of the fugue for organ which made me think of death, no wonder she wouldn't let me drive, delirious delirium is no doubt lucid, doubtless death isn't good for thinking unless you desire absolute focus, Cassandra didn't, her father had died seven years before, is the number seven significant, not like eight I figured, because her father was still alive then, only met him once, he didn't say much, Cassandra did all the chatting, we spoke of nothing I can remember.

I wanted to drive the dream truck, wanted her to relax on the seat, in a word wanted her, she didn't want, didn't ask why, we had gone too far or not far enough for that, she said it was his truck, he wouldn't appreciate that, she drove on, everything in control, until we had a flat, nothing climactic as a blowout, we discovered it when we drove out of her father's driveway, I wanted to change the tire, not with your arm she pointed out, I hadn't noticed, there was no cast on it, it was a dream remember, probably shouldn't try changing tires, never was good at changing anyway, Cassandra insisted on changing it, got out, opened the trunk, pulled out the tools, it started to rain, I could see her arms flailing, rain flicking from long fingered hands, she struggled, she lugged, she changed it in record time. I slunk down in the seat, hid under the floorboards, she climbed into the truck, she was soaking, the old leather interior was wet from her drippings, I should clarify this dreamy moisture as raindrops, after which nothing at all happened except a change in the relationship.

I stopped participating in the inner dream, left Cassandra right there, went to the outer dream, she began to cry, I apologized, she cried harder, I told her I couldn't be blamed for this nightmare, she cried hardest, she shifted gears, perhaps it wasn't even my dream, maybe I was but a minor character in *her* dream, I've disfigured it, with words and commas—changed after all.

I throw out a handful of commas, grab them to drag myself along, long ago I scouted over this blank terrain, planting markers in advance, wanted to plot a course,

course a plot, not all sprouted, when I come to empty spaces I pluck commas from my pockets, toss them out into the immediate future like little progressive notes, I get down on hands and knees to pull myself along, it seems to work, it's always worked before, why not now, except my pockets were empty.

I stand to face the wind and rain blowing all the unrooted markers back toward my face, I can't see in a blizzard of commas, no foresight hindsight says, nearsighted I am, farsighted I'll never be, there must be a way to get through this version, achieving aesthetic distance without another step.

Ancient Tragic Motif as Reflected in the Modern

Aesthetically speaking, it is largely due to Aeschylus and Abner Doubleday that I fell in love with Cassandra. Aeschylus added the second actor to Greek drama in the 5th century B.C., I was not compelled to wander crisscross across America, gathering material, even foolishly hoping to compose an epic of Homeric proportions. Instead, I discovered the second actor, a discovery of the highest rank, making possible the phenomenon of meeting Cassandra in this version.

As legend has it, Doubleday invented baseball at Cooperstown, New York, in 1839. No doubt tinkering with a rule book, if there ever was a chance of it. Teams formed and challenged other teams, these challenges drew crowds, the crowds fell into rank choruses of yeas and boos, the choruses were composed of fans, they still are, Cassandra and I met as baseball fans, but not at Cooperstown.

Chance and luck—possibly fate and destiny—were also elements in our meeting. In this chance meeting, good luck was disguised as bad luck, only to become bad luck later. These are terms from Doubleday's old-fashioned vernacular. Fate and destiny are also old-fashioned, but more antiquated in Greek drama. Aeschylus' terms may be cosmic extensions of Doubleday's, or Abner's terms are humble modifications of the former. There's likely no mention of Greek tragedies on Doubleday's reading list, perhaps he had no reading list, it's no wonder he talked about luck and chance—even legendary figures must come to terms, his terms were simple, the terms of tragedy are simple, the play's the thing, play ball. Is that a cathartic collision at the plate or just bad luck due to chance? Therein lies the question. The chance was a hard foul off the bat of Duke Snider, he's not as legendary as Doubleday or Babe Ruth, but a legend in my lineup. He's not mythical like Aeschylus' Cassandra, Duke was real, my Cassandra was real, that bit of bad luck was real. Fate came in during those early innings, I dropped the foul ball, hardly cruel fate, except I broke my arm.

My fate became Cassandra's destiny, she caught the ball as it rebounded off my left arm, perhaps I have my terms out of order, this happens when you borrow terms from different sources, if a batter bats out of order he's out, must stick to the lineup card, it's not a script, the lineup can do several things but players must walk to the plate in the prearranged order, you see fate gets into everything, Aeschylus had his Zeus, Doubleday had the umpires, I had my Cassandra, but I'm off base, could dive back, but they have me out by a mile, picked off base, sent to the showers, retired to the wings, my destiny was losing Cassandra.

Let me get back to the plate, the bad luck was breaking my arm, more bad luck was dropping the ball, perhaps all that bad luck was good luck in disguise, neither of us was in disguise, this was not a Greek tragedy, good luck in disguise because I fell into her box seat, good luck because she knew what to do, she was a nurse wearing a petticoat, wrapped it around a splint made from our scorecards, we hadn't kept score, it was nothing to nothing at the time, I'd gone to see Snider play his last season, I broke my arm trying to catch his foul tip, made a fair try at it, had it until I cracked my arm on her box seat, the ball and I fell into her lap, good luck, no it was fate by then, I was in Cassandra's care, a great future was predicted for us. Cassandra predicted the broken left arm would heal fine, it didn't, but I chose to stay in the stands, I never leave a ballgame before it's completed, it's my aesthetic, I feel the responsibility to wait it out, it's sometimes a tedious aesthetic, it might even be called a lower class ethics, but Cassandra insisted, I needed to have a proper splint, I believed her, I let go of my aesthetic, I had to, I always held it in my left hand, my left hand was numb, she held my right hand, we left in an ambulance, as far as I know the score never changed, perhaps that game is still going on, destiny arrives in extra innings, I don't know how it will end, we know how tragedies will end, this must not be a tragedy, I was no hero, could a broken arm possibly be a tragic flaw, the score continues in a deadlock, only Zeus can break it, only gods can end it, but there are no gods, the game goes on, we pray for rain (but to whom?).

 With no *deus ex machina* to run red lights, we took the ambulance, Euripides might have got us there a little faster, I never trusted last-chance invocations of the Muse, never trusted her, she never came on time, I never use *never* guardedly enough, must have been delirious, I forgot to guard against everything, I'm never on guard when I'm delirious, there was no need to be on guard, I trusted Cassandra, I believe she recited the Hippocratic oath, I think I heard it, also heard sirens, Odysseus heard sirens, I wondered if Cassandra was a siren, I don't think so, sirens wail, Cassandra wasn't wailing, she was very calm, she placed a damp cloth on my forehead, she knelt at my side all the way, I asked for water and she gave me water, I asked for the Hippocratic oath, she recited the oath, I believed her, she didn't have to be under oath, I was under sedation, I must have fallen asleep. Awake the hospital looked like every hospital, I was delirious, what else could I expect, didn't like hospitals any more than ambulances, never wanted to arrive at a hospital that way again, never trusted doctors, perhaps this was just another delirious hypothesis, the Greeks loved their hypotheses but they should balance, this one doesn't, was there a fat-assed god at the other end of the seesaw throwing all of this out of balance?

    Deliriously I called for Cassandra, without her there's no dialogue, was muttering poetry, I can mutter it only when delirious or drunk, not my own poetry, I don't own any poetry, only borrow it, never borrow my own, I give it away, no one takes it, that's a contradiction, my tongue curls back on itself, it curls back on Cassandra's tongue, we must have been kissing in the hospital, I felt closer to heaven than ever before, that's my synopsis, it's too late for a synopsis, a synopsis shouldn't be full of questions, never trusted synopses, just look how it's spelled, as silly as hypothesis or hypotheses, would never have used any of these words had I not been delirious.

Foot Pedal Notes

Prelude

Once had several scraps of paper, each scrap with a heading, each heading the name for a part of the *baroque fugue*, had the stack of scraps in the correct order, dropped it accidentally, it reshuffled itself, I hadn't numbered the scraps.

Subject

A fugue is a contrapuntal composition, generally in three or four voices, in which a theme or subject of strongly marked character pervades the entire work, entering now in one coordinated voice, now in another—a fugue is on-going, it resists discussion, it rejects definition, this isn't a fugue, this isn't even the subject, the subject is invariably stated alone at the outset in one voice, usually a voice in pain if its arm is broken, then imitated by other voices in close succession.

Counter-Subject

Cassandra drove her father's dreary truck, we were going to visit his grave, graves are plots for the dead, they are strict in form, subject is stated alone on the headstone, we never found it, don't like plots, fortunately we didn't bring flowers that hot day. Fathers die, it's a fact of death, everyone rots eventually, to rot is no small matter, and I never meant to hurt her, believe me, yet my arm still aches.

Answer
　　None yet. Keep playing.

Episodes
　　These, as in *a continuo* . . .

Stretto
　　A fugue is a state of amnesia during which a patient seems to behave in an irrational way—until returning to what's called *normal consciousness* (but should be called *average awareness*)—unable to recall the time period or what transpired, which they call a fugue state or a flight from reality, a fine thing to call it, how can reality be fled from, it's everywhere and everything at once.

Climax
　　You must wait, patience being almost the art forgetting is, of course you can reshuffle the scraps, they remain scraps, any way you stack them they stack against you, that's not why I'm laughing, don't think I'm laughing in your face, the ideal reader has no face, I have no ideal reader, no readers at all, this laughter hurts no one, fills an empty page, I laugh my last laugh and the silence laughs back.

Pedalpoint
　　I touch your face to see if these words have reached you.

Bridge
　　I haven't discussed opera because I don't know it, you must *attend* an opera to actually discover it, yet I've made

notes on opera, haven't numbered them, no matter if I drop the stack, there's no order, never was any order, I play it by ear.

The Early Years

Monteverdi, the Father of Opera oversees erection of music theater from royal Italian patrons, who attend to all the elements: *Arias*, recitative, marches, ballets, duets, ensembles, choruses, mobs, finales, and applause.

Middle History

Lavish productions in Vienna, Brussels, Warsaw. *Opera Seria*. Famous Venice Opera in flames. Vintage Lully, Purcell, Pergolesi, Gluck. Then in the grand Italian operas of Alessandro Scarlatti, the *Aria* obtains absolute supremacy.

Longest Aria

Brunnhilde's immolation scene in Wagner's *Götterdämmerung* takes over 14 minutes. Brief compared to the longest cadenza in operatic history sung by a tenor named Crevelli in 1815. Crevelli sang just two words for 25 minutes at the Milan Opera. The words were *Felice Ognora*, translated literally as Always happy! Always happy? Two minutes should've been plenty of time to get his point across.

Suspension

But how does opera bring about that suspension of disbelief when overly attired, hefty-bosomed sopranos strut across the boards singing what's too trivial to say?

Castrato

Adult male singer with a soprano or contralto voice. How is it done? By means of an operation on the genital organs before puberty. Why? This prevents the high voice from breaking. The singer combines a boy's range with the power of a man. When was this common? During the 17th and 18th centuries, which I think we call *The Gelded Age*. Do note that the part of the Don in *Don Giovanni* was *always* sung by a baritone.

Modern Opera

German Romanticism—Wagner and Nietzsche as *guerre des bouffons*; Rossini composes *Barber of Seville* in bed; *Boris Godounov* and *Madam Butterfly*; Donizetti and Strauss; *The Rape of Lucretia* and *The Rake's Progress*, which did *not* feature Don Juan, alas.

Language Problems

I would settle for a recording of *Don Juan*, except it must be sung in Italian, *obbligato* for Mozart's opera. But my Italian is, well, *non troppo*. However, I take heart since by listening to opera in Italian, an ordinary guy called Joe Green can become a famous composer named Giuseppe Verdi.

Fantasies of a Seducer

I seek the companionship of women, do nothing else, one must *not* be too well adjusted for such activity—a touch of madness is sexy.

I wish *R*'s mouth were not so ravishing, floating upon her face free of any context—a warm, delicate creature with a beautiful life of its own.

M loves wet kisses, but her husband no longer gives her wet kisses. Her lips, no I don't want you to think about her lips, just imagine the lips you desire, these will be her lips, you can't have them, I can't have them again, she has them now, her husband places dry kisses upon them, she was once willing, but now no more.

S smokes with such incredible precision that cigarettes seem extensions of her fingers. Yet this was learned, it was someone's style of smoking, perhaps a montage of movie stars, her smoking just a first step in the seduction, it becomes my member, she never knows this, at least she doesn't act as if she knows this, if you make no connections between these pieces, I'm *not* sorry, I refuse to apologize for my simple alphabet.

No matter how hard I tried to arrive later than *N*, I came earlier, she always arrived later, entering with cavalier calm, no apologies, not even humorously saying good afternoon when we were to meet in the morning, she smiles innocently, says let's get on with it, no small talk today, I haven't a moment to waste.

L seems enchanted by eyes, always staring into the eyes of her lovers, unfortunately sunglasses are mandatory for this loose life, not only in daylight, also at night, this night when I pull them from her face.

Last week *O* said you have rediscovered me, I want to meet you all over again, I had no response, she spoke before I could break off the affair, I was her tongue-tied boy, caressing my face down into her swamp of discovery.

I have a detailed Disclaimer and Release of Responsibility form for the signature of all my subsequent mistress candidates, but before I can show it, V laments that she's too fat to have an affair.

I have not seen *E* in a decade, when I do think of her I feel like an old man who has long outlived her, all I recall now are her calloused palms, had to be sandpapered, also her feet that kicked up their pungent smell, this I remember without malice, those very areas of her anatomy drew me immediately with the strangest sense of pleasure.

I want what you are *C*, although I want what you are *not* also, but that you cannot be, and if you could be, I could not have you—ah fantasy, you are so lovely! Alas reality, you are not lovely enough.

Ending up in a bar alone, not unusual in this loose life, I'm talking to the barkeep, she knows me, I used to meet *Z* here, I could call her, she lives nearby, first met her here, she's a regular, I'm not a regular Don, I don't seduce once, I'm Postmodern, I seduce twenty times, then like Don Juan I leave, never to return before the light fades, I've reached my alphabet's end, I don't have the heart to use numbers, the old barkeep has my number and when she winks I dash from the bar.

I think I will throw myself off a bridge, the throwing is the problem, do I grab the seat of my trousers and heave, perhaps I need only to fall, yet in order to fall I must climb over the railing. Standing on tip toes, leaning forward I see over the edge—a dirty bridge over a polluted river, my hands get soiled by the railing, I take a handkerchief, what a word, it becomes as dirty as my hands, I ball it up, throw it over the rail. The forlorn piece opens up like a miniature parachute, sails a long way down toward the gray river, almost like a pure idea afloat on the dirty water, except it's also dirty, yet from this height it seems relatively clean, relatively clean on an absolutely dirty river. I'm impressed by its ability to float, but suddenly it goes under.

Fugue State

I hitched across the country in my youth, a budding poet gathering images, crossed America countless times, getting rides was easy, I was young, I was clean-cut, I was sincere, I had this handicap, a broken left arm that never healed correctly, it still bends crookedly at the elbow, no one mocks me, sometimes I'm pitied, I desired no pity, just wanted rides.

I wandered like a Beat Poet behind the beat, I heard America singing, I had keen hearing, I played everything by ear, east to the Village, west to San Fran, whatever the traffic would bear, always by chance, saw visions through windshields, blessed and cursed, talked and was silent, I was given advice, I avoided giving advice, I was asked to settle arguments, avoided arguments, I was no mediator, and when a driver suggested I get out, I was stranded in the desert.

I waited twenty hours before a truck stopped, probably he saw my arm, I smiled, he didn't smile back, I nodded, I cleared my throat, I climbed up into the massive cab of the truck, he stepped on the gas, my thumb was nearly knocked off trying to board, my A-number-one-thumb, I could've been dragged across the western deserts, I held on to the swinging door, wouldn't let go, it wouldn't close, the driver reached over and closed us, I scrambled onto the seat, dusted myself off, massaged my thumb, braced my feet under the dashboard, began to relax, locked the door.

I looked at the driver, thanks I said smiling, he looked straight ahead, I relaxed a bit less, roar inside the cab overwhelming, perhaps he never heard me, what difference I thought, the day was going, how could we go on forever without refueling, driving due west the sky was mauve then burnt orange then smoky, and finally black.

I couldn't see the gas gauge, already it seemed an interminable drive, how far did he expect to drive, what was our destination—no destination except reaching the point when fuel was exhausted, that point like any other—no point, this was endless desert, couldn't distinguish objects, only the rectangle of concrete falling under beams of light, muted engine roar, tires swooshing on pavement, that hum of insects.

Where in hell are we going? But no answer, not a word.

He steered with both hands, wheel once hot and sticky now cool and dry, green speedometer glaring, couldn't decipher it, driver never glanced my way, kept staring straight through the windshield, perhaps he was only afraid to veer off course, no doubt he was a safe driver in full command, I stared as his facial muscles twitched, I think he was smiling, large hands strangling the steering wheel, his massive knuckles were white.

Fugue refuses definition, cannot be evoked in words, nothing else can be a fugue, not even this wandering journey, a fugue flies through its own consciousness, its own desert, its own fugue state—it can contradict itself, overtake itself, leave itself behind, but never end, perpetual music, instruments follow, ears go on alone, hearing becomes the final arbiter, but even hearing fools itself. I knew I'd never hitch again.

Interview with a Pianist

Sir, is it true you play the piano no longer?
No longer, no shorter, but certainly I play.
I live across the courtyard but never hear you.
When are you there?
All day.
You never get out?
Yes, but mostly during evenings.
I play every evening.
May I listen one evening?

If you wish.
Tonight?
Yes, but only from across the courtyard.
Why not here in your parlor?
I no longer perform.
But you still play, isn't that correct?
Yes. I play every evening, but I no longer perform.
You play only for yourself?
Yes.
What is your repertoire?
Always the same music.
Which music?
Für Elise.
Exclusively?
I haven't the range for anything more.
I used to play that Beethoven ditty as a student.
So did I, and I remain a student.
But *Für Elise* seems like child's play.
I try to be childlike while playing.
I see.
Would you care to try it?
A rank amateur sitting at a master's concert grand?
It's only a baby grand, be my guest.
Oh no, no thank you, Sir.
Whatever you wish.
I wish you would play.
I will, I always do—at evening.
But only *Für Elise*?
Actually, only the first nine notes.
Only nine notes?
Do you remember those notes?
I could read them.

I no longer have the music here.
But Sir, I have no wish to play in any case.
It would be impossible to play them perfectly.
I'm certain with enough practice one could do it.
Yes, of course—practice, a lifetime of practice.
A lifetime for only the first nine notes?
Yes.
Are not some of those nine notes repeated?
Yes.
And are not all played by the right hand.
Precisely.
Because you no longer use the left hand?
I use it, but never at the keyboard.
Yet, I've never heard you play a note.
Music will drift to your courtyard this evening.
Why only evenings?
A melancholic holdover from concertizing, I suspect.
But you will never perform again?
There's no point.
But you will go on playing?
Yes, every evening, I play my nine notes.
I'll be listening.
You must listen carefully.
I shall listen carefully.
The notes are played softly.
Yes.
Very softly.
Yes.
I play them only once.

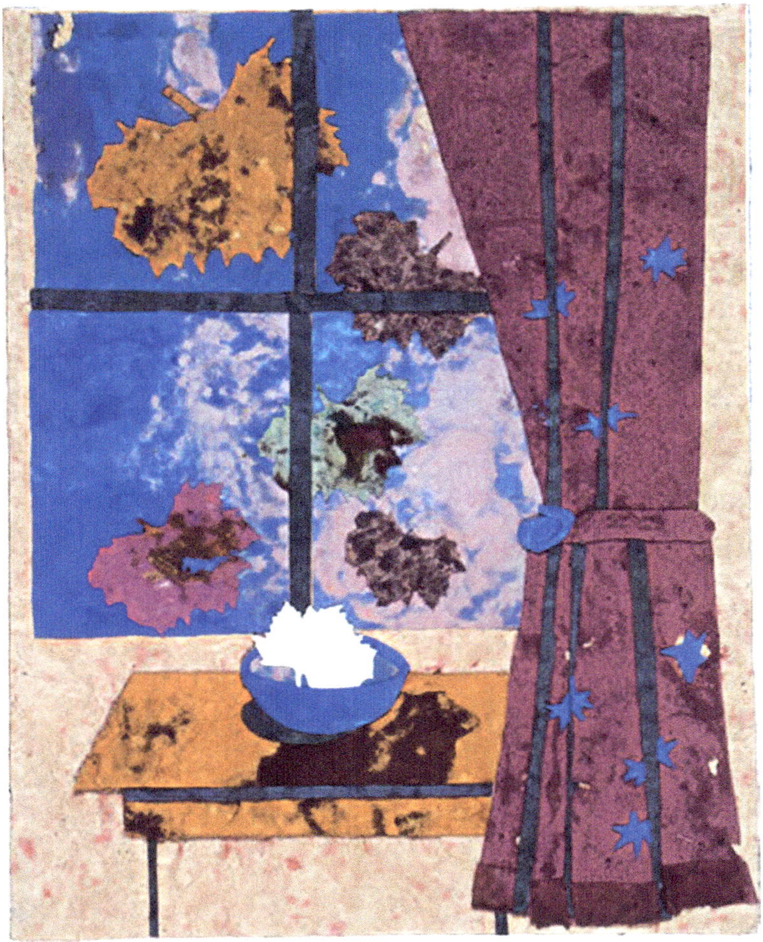

CPSIA information can be obtained
at www.ICGtesting.com
Printed in the USA
FSOW03n1214260216
17234FS